To Adam, our sweetheart,
with love, hugs and kisses from
Mum, Dad, Harry, Robbie and Molly.

Adam is an angel and lives on a cloud
and makes his Mummy and Daddy so proud.
With long golden hair you just could not miss,
he always has time for a hug and a kiss.
The message he sends from his cloud every day,
is to spend more time with each other and play.
The most important thing in life is this,
show your love for your family with a hug and a kiss.

Written by Benji Bennett.
benji@adamsprintingpress.ie

Illustrations by Roxanne Burchartz of Cartoon Saloon.
www.cartoonsaloon.ie

Designed by Bold.
www.reallybold.com

ISBN 978-1-906818-02-9

Published by

Adam's Printing Press is dedicated to spreading Adam's message of the importance of love, laughter and play within the family
and will make a donation from the proceeds of all books published under its imprint to children's charities.

Adam's Printing Press
PO Box 11379, Blackrock, Co. Dublin, Ireland
Email: info@adamsprintingpress.ie
Web: www.adamsprintingpress.ie
Tel: +353 1 2833620

A donation of 2% of the recommended retail price of this book will go to

Make-A-Wish Foundation® International has approved this promotion and is very grateful to Adam's Printing Press for their support of our
mission, which is to grant the wishes of children with life-threatening medical conditions to enrich the human experience with hope, strength and joy.
For more information, please visit www.worldwish.org

It's time to sleep but before you go, there is I love you much more than a Christmas Eve night, I love you much more than the elves clever tricks,

something I really want you to know.
when Santa makes Rudolph's red nose shine so bright.
used to make presents that every child picks.

Adam sat down late on Christmas Eve night
And wrote to ask Santa to bring him a kite

A bat and a ball for Harry and Robbie
And a princess' dress for his
Sweet sister Molly.

With Christmas so close Jack Frost nipped at his nose
So he asked for some slippers to warm up his toes.

Then Adam put on his red Christmas Eve sweater
And thought about how to deliver his letter.

"Huff puff I love you Fluff, there's something that I need,

"I have an idea," Adam thought to himself,
"I'll deliver my letter to Santa's chief elf."

So he called out for Fluff his magical cloud,
By closing his eyes and saying out loud,

Then Fluff arrived with big Fluffy kisses
And flew Adam to Santa the night before Christmas.

With snow on the ground and frost in the air
They flew through the night and soon they were there.

A lift to Santa's North Pole on your back with lightning speed. "

"We're here! We're here!" Adam said with a cheer
But was met by sad faces on the elves and reindeer.

"Adam," they said, "we have terrible news,
Rudolph is sick and Santa's the blues.

There's no Christmas magic to light Rudolph's nose
And he can't fly the sleigh unless it brightly glows."

"Don't worry," said Adam, "I'll make you all proud
I'll find you some magic with Fluffy my cloud."

The elves got to work loading up Santa's sleigh
While Adam flew off to save Christmas Day.

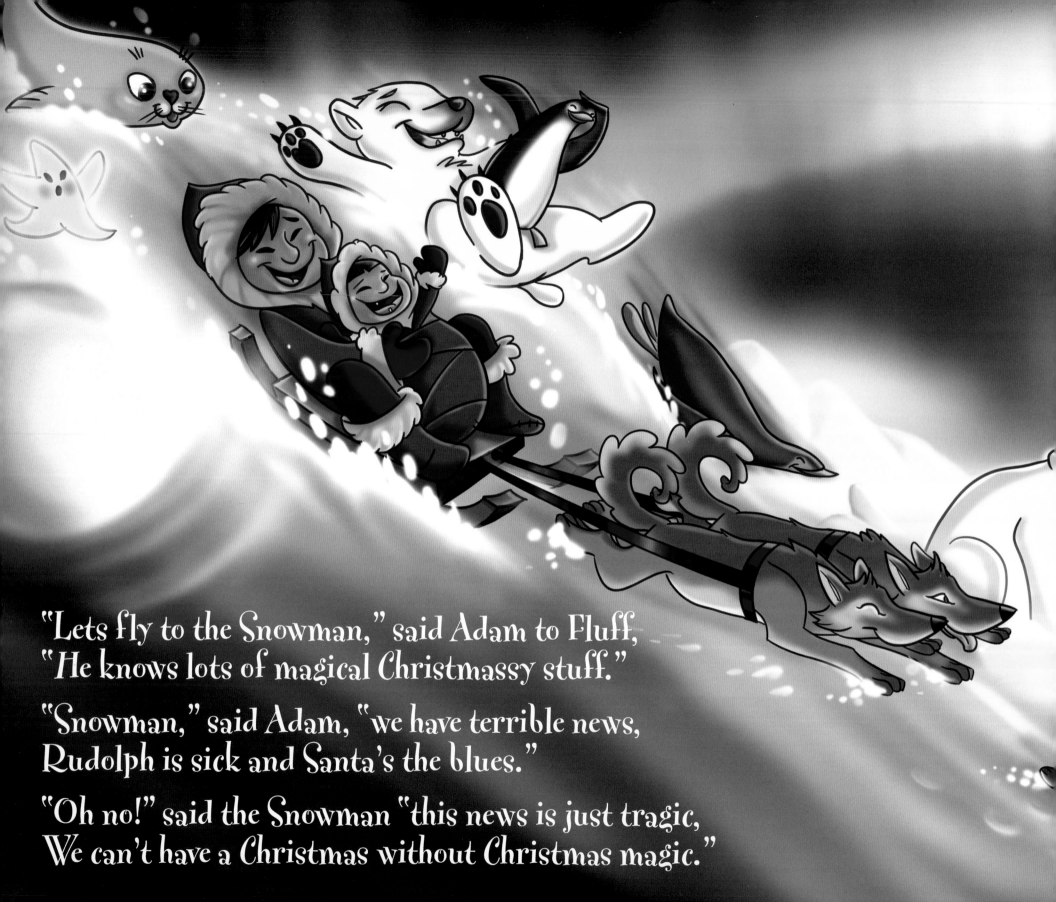

"Lets fly to the Snowman," said Adam to Fluff,
"He knows lots of magical Christmassy stuff."

"Snowman," said Adam, "we have terrible news,
Rudolph is sick and Santa's the blues."

"Oh no!" said the Snowman "this news is just tragic,
We can't have a Christmas without Christmas magic."

Snowman hugged Adam then hopped onto Fluff
And gave him some magic but it was not enough.

"I know," said the Snowman, "who'll give us some more
The Christmas tree angel has magic galore."

"Look!" Adam shouted, "I think I can see
A love angel on top of that big Christmas tree.

Oh beautiful angel can you help us please
And give us the magic of Christmassy trees.

We need it to light up poor Rudolph's red nose
Coz he can't fly the sleigh unless it brightly glows."

"Adam" she said, "I think I just could
Give you some magic coz you are so good."

She gave him some love but twas still not enough
So to help Snowman and Adam she jumped onto Fluff.

As the magic of Christmas was starting to grow
They flew to Red Robin down on the snow.

"We heard that when baby Jesus was born
The fire made your red breast when you kept him warm."

"Red Robin," said Adam, "Santa's sleigh will not go
Without the magic we need to make Rudolph's nose glow."

"Oh no!" said Red Robin, "we cannot have this,"
Then gave Adam a magical Christmassy kiss.

With time running out Robin flew onto Fluff
Who flew them away with a huff and a puff.

Fluff flew to the manger as fast as he could
To Edgar the donkey who was both kind and good.

"Edgar," said Adam, "we need your help fast
Without it this Christmas just might be our last."

"Oh no!" Edgar said, who was in some distress,
"I've no Christmas magic just love and kindness."

Adam, the Angel, Red Robin and Snowman
Said, "don't worry, Edgar, we're sure that we can

Use kindness and love to fill Santa's sleigh
With the magic we need to save Christmas day."

With Edgar on board Adam said with a shout,
"We must get to Santa before time runs out."

With the magic they needed to save Christmas Day
Fluff flew as fast as he could all the way to the sleigh.

Over the rooftops late on Christmas Eve
They all crossed their fingers then could not believe

When they saw in the distance the elves and reindeer
Dancing and singing, " It's Adam, he's here."

When Fluff landed Adam down onto the snow
He was surrounded by a magical Christmassy glow.

"Adam," said Santa, "we've no time to lose
Did you get any Christmassy magic to use

To make Rudolph's nose shine Christmassy bright
So we can deliver the presents tonight."

"Yes," replied Adam, "but what do I do
To get all of the magic from me into you?"

"Adam," said Santa, "that bit is so easy
Just give poor old Rudolph a hug and a squeezy."

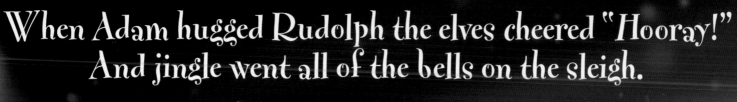

When Adam hugged Rudolph the elves cheered "Hooray!"
And jingle went all of the bells on the sleigh.

"I cannot believe it I have my glow back,"
Said Rudolph as Santa grabbed his Christmas toy sack.

The elves all lined up for the take-off parade
As a final check of the list was being made.

"Ho! Ho!" shouted Santa, "we have so much to do"
And with the magic of Christmas away the sleigh flew.

Never before on a Christmas Eve night
Had Rudolph's red nose ever glowed quite so bright.

As Santa flew off with the toys on the sled
He used magic to put Fluff and Adam to bed.

And later as Adam slept soundly that night
Santa brought him a truly magnificent kite.

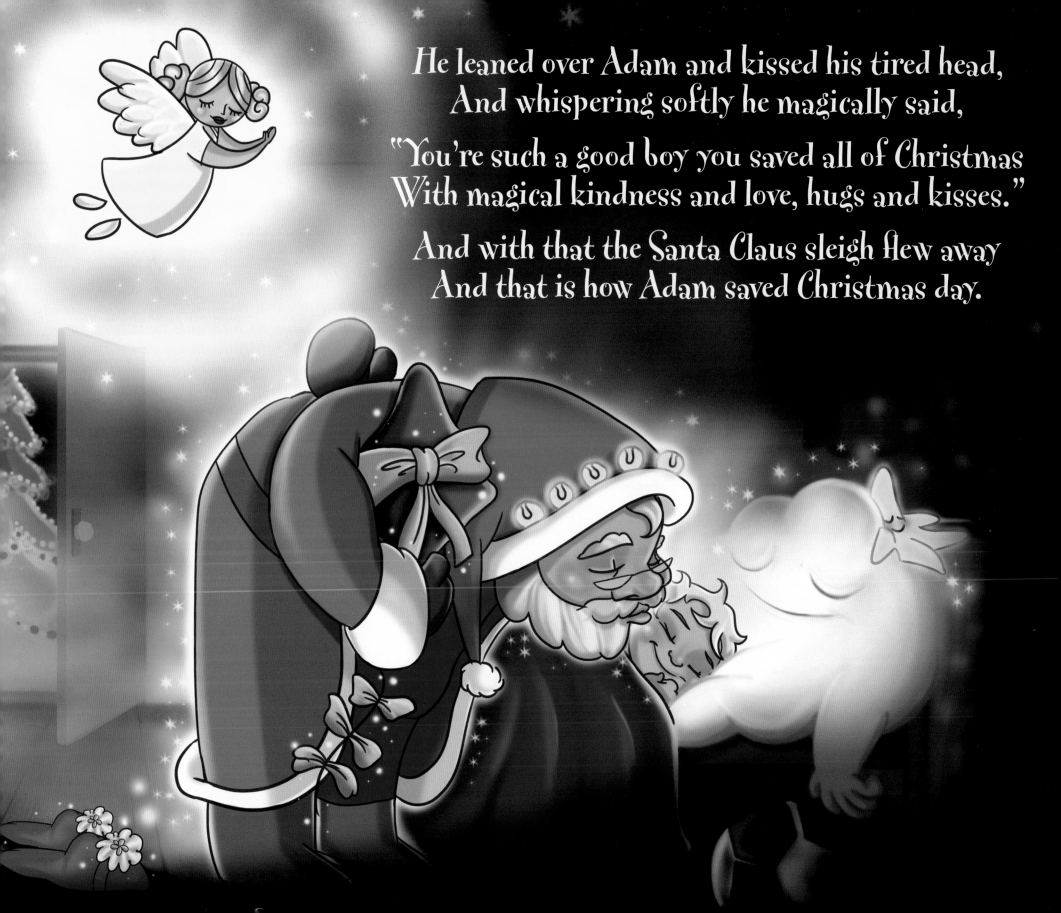

He leaned over Adam and kissed his tired head,
And whispering softly he magically said,

"You're such a good boy you saved all of Christmas
With magical kindness and love, hugs and kisses."

And with that the Santa Claus sleigh flew away
And that is how Adam saved Christmas day.

It's time to sleep my bundle of joy
I love you much more than a Christmas Day toy
Even much more than a Christmas Eve night
Sweet Dreams my love I kiss you good night.